5-15

DATE

6-4-15
7-23-15
8-11-15
11-4-15
JUL 17 2017

WITHDRAWN

BRODART, CO.

Welcome to Royal Prep

Written by Lisa Ann Marsoli
Illustrated by Character Building Studio
and the Disney Storybook Artists

WWW.ABDOPUBLISHING.COM

Reinforced library bound edition published in 2015 by Spotlight, a division of ABDO
PO Box 398166, Minneapolis, Minnesota 55439. Spotlight produces high-quality reinforced library
bound editions for schools and libraries. Published by agreement with Disney Enterprises, Inc.

Printed in the United States of America, North Mankato, Minnesota.
052014   072014

Disney PRESS
New York

THIS BOOK CONTAINS
RECYCLED MATERIALS

CATALOGING-IN-PUBLICATION DATA

Marsoli, Lisa Ann.
 Sofia the first: welcome to Royal Prep / written by Lisa Ann Marsoli ; illustrated by Character Building
Studio and Disney Storybook Artists.
   p. cm. -- (World of reading. Level 1)
Summary: It's open house at Royal Prep! Will Sofia and her friends get everything ready in time?
1. Princesses--Juvenile fiction. 2. Preparatory schools--Juvenile fiction. I. Character Building Studio, ill.
II. Disney Storybook Artists, ill. III. Title. IV. Series. V. Sofia the first (Television program)
[Fic]--dc23

978-1-61479-252-9   (Reinforced Library Bound Edition)

Spotlight
A Division of ABDO
www.abdopublishing.com

Open House at Royal Prep
is almost here!
Sofia can't wait!

The fairies give everyone a job.

Sofia, Hildegard, and Khalid
clean and stack and tidy.

Jin and James decorate
from top to bottom.

Clio and Jun help bake the snacks.
Amber and Maya water and sweep.

Next the children practice
for the Open House show.
They go over their dance steps.
They read poems.

They sing and play songs.
They want the show to be perfect.

Finally, the children choose
their best artwork.
"This is Cedric, the royal
sorcerer," James says.

"Once, he used magic
and turned himself into
a mushroom!"
Sofia picks a wall hanging.
Amber can't decide what to show.

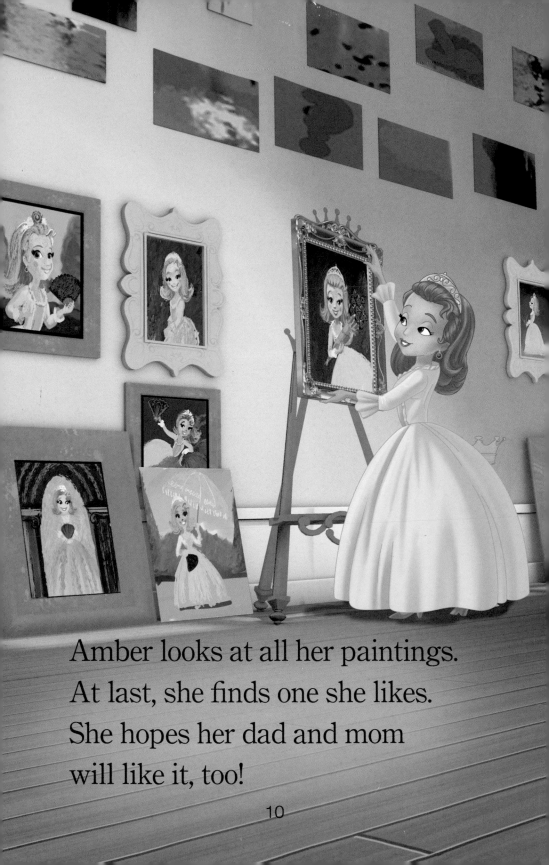

Amber looks at all her paintings.
At last, she finds one she likes.
She hopes her dad and mom
will like it, too!

10

After Amber leaves,
Sofia spots some jars of paint.
"Can you help me put these
away?" she asks James.

James picks up the jars.
They start to slip.
"Uh-oh!" he cries.
Paint flies everywhere!

"Amber is going to be so mad at me!" cries James. Sofia and James try to wipe away the paint.

They make the mess worse!
The painting is ruined!
"We can't tell Amber," says James.

"I'm going to switch the paintings,"
James says.

"It won't work," says Sofia.

"Amber picked that painting
just for Mom and Dad."

James finds a blank canvas.
He copies the painting he ruined.
It looks terrible!

James still wants to fix his mistake.
He opens the windows wide.

"I'll say the wind
blew the painting over!" he says.
"Why don't you just tell the truth?"
asks Sofia.

"Tell the truth about what?"
asks Amber.
She looks at Sofia and James.
She sees her ruined painting!

"I'm sorry," James says.
"It was an accident."
"What will I show Mom and Dad
at Open House?" cries Amber.
"That was my best painting."

Later, Sofia has an idea.
She shares it with Amber.
"Do you think our parents
will like it?" Amber asks.
"They will love it!" Sofia says.

Amber goes to work.
She stays out of sight.
She wants to surprise King
Roland and Queen Miranda.

Sofia and James help Amber
with the painting.

At last, it is finished!

Flora, Fauna, and Merryweather welcome everyone to Open House.

Then the children put on their show.

Next it's time to visit each class.

King Roland sees James's statue.

"Look, it's Cedric!" says the king.

"I'd know him anywhere!"

The king and queen
admire Sofia's wall hanging.

Finally, it's time to see Amber's painting. Her parents love it! "It's our first family portrait!" exclaims the queen.

The king and queen

hang the painting in a special place.

Everyone agrees it is

Amber's best yet—even Amber!